Hi! I'm Michelle Tanner. I'm nine years old, and I've got some awesome news. I'm running for fourth-grade class president! There's just one problem. I'm up against Rachel Tilly. She's giving the kids T-shirts and pastries so they'll vote for her. And it's working!

But I'm going to ask my family for some advice. If we all put on our thinking caps I know we can come up with something. That's because we have *a lot* of thinking caps at my house. My family is huge!

There's my dad and my two older sisters, D.J. and Stephanie. But that's not all.

My mom died when I was little. So my uncle Jesse moved in to help Dad take care of us. So did Joey Gladstone. He's my dad's friend from college. It's almost like having three dads. But that's still not all!

First Uncle Jesse got married to Becky Donaldson. Then they had twin boys, Nicky and Alex. The twins are four years old now. And they're so cute.

That's nine people. And our dog, Comet, makes ten. Sure, it gets kind of crazy sometimes. But I wouldn't change it for anything. It's so much fun living in a full house!

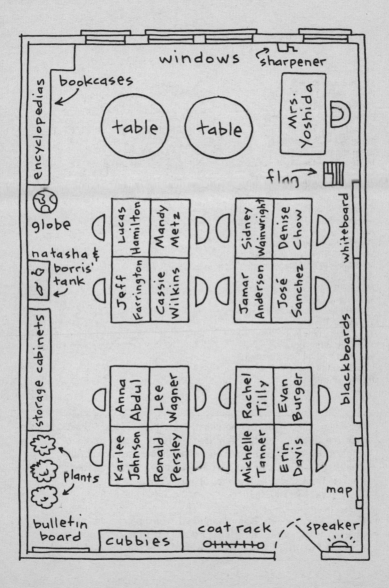

FULL HOUSE™ MICHELLE novels

The Great Pet Project
The Super-Duper Sleepover Party
My Two Best Friends
Lucky, Lucky Day
The Ghost in My Closet
Ballet Surprise
Major League Trouble
My Fourth-Grade Mess
Bunk 3, Teddy and Me
My Best Friend Is a Movie Star!
   (Super Special)
The Big Turkey Escape
The Substitute Teacher
Calling All Planets
I've Got a Secret
How to Be Cool
The Not-So-Great Outdoors
My Ho-Ho-Horrible Christmas
My Almost Perfect Plan
April Fools!
My Life Is a Three-Ring Circus
Welcome to My Zoo
The Problem with Pen Pals
Tap Dance Trouble
The Fastest Turtle in the West
The Baby-sitting Boss
The Wish I Wish I Never Wished
Pigs, Pies, and Plenty of Problems
If I Were President

Activity Books

My Awesome Holiday Friendship Book
My Super Sleepover Book

FULL HOUSE™ SISTERS

Two on the Town
One Boss Too Many

Available from MINSTREL Books

For orders other than by individual consumers, Pocket Books grants a discount on the purchase of **10 or more** copies of single titles for special markets or premium use. For further details, please write to the Vice President of Special Markets, Pocket Books, 1230 Avenue of the Americas, 9th Floor, New York, NY 10020-1586.

For information on how individual consumers can place orders, please write to Mail Order Department, Simon & Schuster Inc., 100 Front Street, Riverside, NJ 08075.

FULL HOUSE™

Michelle

and Friends

IF I WERE PRESIDENT

Judy Katschke

A Parachute Book

A MINSTREL® BOOK

Published by POCKET BOOKS
New York   London   Toronto   Sydney   Tokyo   Singapore

A MINSTREL PAPERBACK *Original*

A Minstrel Book published by
POCKET BOOKS, a division of Simon & Schuster Inc.
1230 Avenue of the Americas, New York, NY 10020

A PARACHUTE BOOK

Copyright © and ™ 1999 by Warner Bros.

FULL HOUSE, characters, names and all related indicia are
trademarks of Warner Bros. © 1999.

ISBN: 0–671–02153–2

First Minstrel Books printing November 1999

10 9 8 7 6 5 4 3 2 1

A MINSTREL BOOK and colophon are registered trademarks of
Simon & Schuster Inc.

Printed in the U.S.A.

IF I WERE PRESIDENT

Chapter

1

♥ "I can't believe it!" Michelle Tanner cried. She bounced in her seat on the school bus. "The Ginger Girls are going to be in San Francisco in three weeks!"

It was Monday morning. Michelle was sitting next to her best friend, Cassie Wilkins. Her other best friend, Mandy Metz, was in the seat right in front of them.

"I'd do anything to get tickets for a Ginger Girls concert," Cassie said.

Mandy leaned over the back of her seat. "Would you put anchovies on your peanut butter sandwich?" she asked.

1

Michelle giggled. Cassie hated anchovies more than anything.

"Gross! No way!" Cassie shook her head. "But I'd do anything else."

Michelle wanted to go to the concert, too. The Ginger Girls were the coolest singing group in the world. They wore awesome clothes, and had fun names like May, Lulu, Gigi, and Tawny.

"Do you think we could get tickets?" Mandy asked.

"It might be hard to get them," Michelle replied. "Everybody wants to go."

"You're right." Cassie sighed. "Besides, Ginger Girls tickets are probably more expensive than gold."

Mandy slumped down in her seat. Michelle and Cassie stared out the window.

"I know!" Mandy popped up again. "What about your uncle Jesse, Michelle? He's a musician. Maybe he knows the Ginger Girls."

Cassie's eyes lit up. "Maybe he can get us tickets!"

Michelle wasn't sure if Uncle Jesse knew the Ginger Girls. But it was worth a try. "I'll ask him tonight at dinner," she promised.

"All right!" Mandy cried. "Michelle's uncle is getting us tickets to the Ginger Girls!"

A group of kids turned and stared at Michelle.

"Maybe," Michelle told them.

The bus hissed to a stop. Al, the bus driver, opened the doors. Three kids stepped into the bus. One of them was Rachel Tilly.

"There's someone who can afford tickets," Cassie whispered.

Michelle nodded. Rachel had just moved to San Francisco with her family. Her father owned bakeries all over the country.

Rachel always wore expensive clothes and carried her books in a real leather backpack. She got straight-A report cards. And she was great at sports. But Michelle knew one thing Rachel wasn't good at—being nice.

"Good morning, everybody," Rachel called out. She stopped in the middle of the aisle. "I have an announcement to make." Rachel flipped her super-long brown hair over her shoulder. "I want to say that—"

"I can't start the bus until everyone is seated," Al called out.

"This will take only a second," Rachel told Al. She turned back to the kids. "Guess what? I'm running for fourth-grade class president."

But the class nominations weren't until tomorrow, Michelle thought. No one was running yet.

Rachel yanked a stack of flyers from her backpack. She started handing them out. "Here, Michelle." Rachel gave her a flyer. "Cassie, Mandy, you can look on."

Michelle and her friends stared at the bright yellow paper. In the middle was a picture of

Rachel. Underneath were the words: Rachel Tilly—For a Better Fourth Grade.

"Well?" Rachel asked Michelle. "What do you think?"

Michelle shook her head. "You can't run for class president until you have three nominations. That's the school rule."

"Three?" Rachel laughed. "I already have *five* kids who promised to vote for me."

Mandy leaned over her seat. "Sure. After Rachel gave them her father's cookies and doughnuts," she whispered to Michelle.

"I heard that, Mandy!" Rachel snapped. When she stopped handing out flyers, she smiled. "Any questions?"

Michelle had one. "If you're elected class president, what will you do for the fourth grade?" she asked Rachel.

"What will I do?" Rachel stared at Michelle. "Hmm. I never thought about that." Then Rachel smiled. "I'll have the whole fourth grade put on a special show at the end of the school year," she said. "It will have the coolest costumes, sets, and a talented star!"

"A star?" Mandy asked. "Who?"

"Me, of course." Rachel stuck her chin in the air. "I take ballet lessons, gymnastics, *and* acting."

Michelle couldn't believe her ears. "All you would do is put on a show?" she asked.

Rachel nodded. "I bet it would fill every seat in the auditorium."

"Great," Al called out. He pointed to the back of the bus. "Now, how about filling one of *those* seats so I can start moving the bus?"

The kids on the bus laughed as Rachel stomped to a seat. She sat down and folded her arms.

Michelle turned to Mandy and Cassie. "That's it?" she whispered. "That's all her campaign is about?"

6

Cassie crumpled Rachel's flyer. "What else do you expect from Rachel?"

"A lot more than that," Michelle said. She shifted the books on her lap. "A good class president can really make a difference."

"How?" Mandy asked.

"Like getting us onto the cool playground— the one the fifth-graders use," Michelle said. "Or helping to organize neat field trips and a big class picnic. Or making the food in the cafeteria better. Or—"

Mandy and Cassie glanced at each other. They started to giggle.

"What?" Michelle asked.

"We know who would make the perfect fourth-grade class president," Mandy said.

"Someone who's nice, smart, and not too shy," Cassie added.

Michelle looked around the bus. "Who?"

Mandy and Cassie pointed to Michelle. *"You!"*

7

Chapter
2

♥ "Did you say *me?*" Michelle asked her friends. "You guys want *me* to run for class president?"

Mandy nodded. "You already have a zillion great ideas."

"But the only time I was ever president was in the second-grade play," Michelle said. "When I played George Washington."

"And you were great," Mandy replied. "Especially when you chopped down that cherry tree."

Cassie touched Michelle's shoulder. "Think about it. Okay?"

Michelle stared out the window as the bus pulled up to the school. She pictured herself giving speeches, planning class picnics, and working for more recess equipment.

"President Michelle Tanner," Michelle whispered. Then she grinned to herself. That sounded pretty good! Maybe I should run for president, she thought. Maybe *I* could be the one to make a difference in the school. Michelle turned to her friends. "I'm going to do it. I'm going to run for fourth-grade president!"

Michelle thought about the election all day at school. When she got home, she couldn't wait to tell her family about her decision. And she had a lot of people to tell.

There was her father, Danny, and her two sisters, Stephanie and D.J. Uncle Jesse and Aunt Becky lived on the third floor with their four-year-old twin boys, Nicky and Alex.

Uncle Joey lived in the basement apartment.

He was Danny's friend from college. He moved in to help out with the family after Michelle's mom died.

Michelle lived in a very full house. That's why she had to wait until dinner to tell everybody her news—when the whole family was together.

"So how was everyone's day?" Danny asked at the dinner table. He passed a plate of chicken to Stephanie.

Michelle opened her mouth to speak. But Stephanie beat her to it.

"Great, Dad." Stephanie grabbed a chicken wing. "I got the lead in the school play."

"Bravo! Bravo!" Uncle Jesse cried.

"Guess what?" D.J. asked. "I've just been made the editor of the college yearbook."

"That's wonderful," Danny said. "Congratulations, D.J."

Michelle tried speaking again. But as soon as she opened her mouth . . .

"News flash!" Joey jumped up from his chair. He pointed to Comet, the family's dog. "Comet learned a new trick today."

Michelle watched as Joey snapped his fingers. Comet barked and rolled over—twice.

"Now, that's a dog who's on a roll." Joey sat down again.

Michelle giggled. Joey was a comedian. He was always joking around. Then she tapped her fork against her glass.

DING! DING! DING!

"May I have everyone's attention please?" Michelle called.

The table grew quiet.

Michelle took a deep breath. "I am running for fourth-grade class president."

"That's awesome," Stephanie said. "But make sure you really want to do it. Being class president is a lot of work."

"That's okay." Michelle smiled. "I'm a very hard worker."

"And a school election can turn into a popularity contest," D.J. warned.

"That will never happen to me," Michelle insisted. "I'm going to win for my ideas. I have lots of them. All I need are three kids to nominate me tomorrow. And I already have two."

"Then I think that deserves a toast," Danny said. He raised his water glass.

"Toast?" Joey asked. "But there's no bread on the table."

"This kind of toast," Danny replied. "To Michelle. You'll make the greatest president the fourth grade has ever seen."

"To President Michelle," D.J. said. "You have my support."

"Mine, too!" Nicky cried.

"Mine three!" Alex shouted.

"Mine four," Stephanie said. "Now, can you please pass the potato salad?"

"Sure," Michelle said with a grin. She handed a big blue bowl to Stephanie.

When everyone was busy eating, Uncle Jesse ran to get his guitar. He came back to the table and rested the guitar on his lap. "I think Michelle's campaign calls for a song," Uncle Jesse said. He strummed his guitar. "Vote for Michelle," he sang. "Because Michelle . . . is swell!"

Michelle clapped to the tune. Soon everyone would find out how swell she really was!

Michelle hummed Uncle Jesse's song the next morning in school. She hung her jacket on a hook in the closet.

"Today's the big day, Michelle," Cassie told her. "When the candidates get nominated."

"Yeah," Mandy said. "Are you ready?"

Michelle was about to answer, when someone tapped her shoulder. She turned and saw José Sanchez.

"Hi, José," Michelle said. "What's up?"

José leaned close to Michelle. "I heard on the bus yesterday that your uncle might be able to get Ginger Girls tickets," he whispered. "They're my favorite group. Can he get me a ticket, too?"

Michelle gave her forehead a little smack. She was so busy talking about the election last night. She forgot to ask Uncle Jesse about the Ginger Girls! "I didn't ask him yet," Michelle admitted. "But I'll talk to him tonight."

"Thanks, Michelle," José said. He walked toward his desk.

"I can't believe I forgot to ask about the tickets," Michelle told Cassie and Mandy. Then she remembered something else. "Uh-oh."

"What?" Cassie asked.

"I need one more fourth-grader to nominate me in assembly today," Michelle said. "I can't run with just two supporters."

Jamar Anderson hung up his jacket next to Michelle's.

"I'll nominate you, Michelle," he said. "You'd make a cool class president."

"Thanks, Jamar!" Michelle said.

After a social studies lesson, the class filed into the auditorium for assembly. They took their usual seats in the fourth and fifth rows. Michelle sat between Cassie and Mandy. Jamar was seated right behind Michelle.

Mr. Posey, the school principal, walked onto the stage. He was wearing a red, white, and blue tie. "Good morning, boys and girls," Mr. Posey said into the microphone.

"Good morning, Mr. Posey," the kids said back.

"Before we begin the nominations for fourth-grade class president," Mr. Posey announced, "I want to tell you that I've invited a very special guest to our assembly in three weeks."

Excited whispers filled the auditorium. Michelle wondered who the guest would be.

"A dentist!" Mr. Posey said with a grin.

The fourth-graders groaned.

Mr. Posey raised both hands. "And . . . he'll be passing out tubes of bubble-gum-flavored toothpaste!"

Everyone clapped.

"Who cares about the toothpaste?" Mandy whispered. "Let's get to the nominations."

"Now," Mr. Posey said, rubbing his hands. "I'm sure you're all itching to begin the nominations."

Michelle felt as if she had butterflies in her stomach. She wanted to run for class president more than anything.

"Do we have any nominations?" Mr. Posey asked.

Sidney Wainwright jumped up from her seat. "I nominate Rachel Tilly!"

Michelle glanced over at Sidney. Rachel and Sidney were becoming good friends— ever since Rachel came to Fraser Street Elementary.

Rachel pretended to act surprised. "Me?" She gasped. "I can't believe it. No way!"

"She's such a faker," Cassie whispered.

"Does anyone else nominate Rachel?" Mr. Posey asked.

"I do," Ron Persley said.

"So do I!" a voice called out.

Michelle froze in her seat. That voice sounded familiar. It sounded like . . . like . . .

She spun around and gasped.

It was Jamar Anderson!

Chapter
3

♥ Michelle stared at Jamar. How could he nominate Rachel? she wondered. Jamar said he would nominate her!

"That makes three," Mr. Posey said. "Rachel Tilly is in the race."

Michelle leaned over the back of her seat. "You were supposed to nominate *me*," Michelle whispered.

"I know," Jamar whispered back. "But Rachel gave me a whole bunch of jelly doughnuts." He unzipped his backpack and pointed to a white paper bag. "They're apple cinnamon. My favorite!"

Michelle sank back into her seat. I have only two supporters again, she thought glumly. What will I do now?

"Are there any other nominations?" Mr. Posey asked.

A boy in another fourth-grade class stood up. "I think Victor Velez would make a great president."

"Me, too!" a girl shouted.

"Victor for president," another boy called out.

Mr. Posey smiled. "Victor Velez is in the race."

Michelle knew Victor from Mrs. Barnett's class. "Victor?" she asked. "But he's so quiet and shy."

"Maybe he's not as shy as we thought," Cassie said.

Mr. Posey put his hands on his hips. He looked around the auditorium. "Anyone else?"

Mandy stood up. "I nominate Michelle Tanner for class president."

"Me, too," Cassie said, jumping up.

Michelle listened for another nomination. "Please . . . please . . . please . . ."

"Remember, boys and girls," Mr. Posey said. "Michelle needs *three* fourth-graders to nominate her."

The auditorium was as quiet as a library. Then a girl in the fifth row called out, "I nominate Michelle, too."

Michelle glanced over her shoulder. Erin Davis was smiling and raising her hand. Erin sat across from Michelle in Mrs. Yoshida's class.

Michelle grinned from ear to ear. She had three whole supporters now. And that meant *she* was in the race!

"You did it, Michelle," Cassie said later in the lunchroom. "You're running for class president."

Michelle took a bite of her sliced hot dog

and sauerkraut sandwich. "The election is next Tuesday," she said. "I have a week to talk about my ideas with the other kids."

Cassie leaned over the table. "You know, Michelle," she said. "Now that you're a candidate, you're going to need Mandy and me more than ever."

"I know," Michelle nodded. "Friends are important at a time like this."

Cassie and Mandy looked at each other and grinned.

"So are campaign managers," Cassie said.

"Campaign managers?" Michelle repeated.

Mandy gave the table a little whack. "To make sure you have the best campaign ever!"

"We can paint a big banner with your name on it," Cassie suggested. "Hand out lots of candy. Get your picture in the school paper—"

Michelle formed the letter T with her hands. "Time out, you guys. I don't want this to be a popularity contest," Michelle said. "I want to win because the kids like my ideas."

Mandy pouted. "But that's boring."

"Oh, yeah?" Michelle said. "Just watch." She turned to the other kids at the table. "Hey, everybody. How would you like more books in the school library? And videos?"

Lucas Hamilton looked up from his tuna sandwich.

"Videos?" he asked. "Cool!"

Michelle picked up a packet of ketchup. "Ketchup is great on French fries," she said. "But it's no good with tacos. I think we need to get packets of salsa in the lunchroom, too."

"Chunky?" Anna Abdul asked.

Michelle grinned. *Extra*-chunky!"

More kids crowded around Michelle to listen.

"If I'm elected president, I'll make sure there are more jump ropes during recess,"

Michelle said. "And kick balls, too. I'll even—"

"Hey, you guys," Lucas interrupted. He pointed over Michelle's shoulder. "Look what Rachel's doing."

"Wow!" Anna cried. "Let's check it out."

Michelle's jaw dropped as the kids left the table. Where was everyone going? Michelle stared across the lunchroom and frowned.

Rachel was passing out black T-shirts. The words VOTE FOR RACHEL were spelled out on them in silver and gold glitter.

That's not fair, Michelle thought. Rachel is trying to win votes with T-shirts—not ideas.

A group of fourth-graders walked by carrying Rachel's shirts.

"These rock," one boy said.

"I'm going to vote for Rachel," a girl added. "She's cool."

"Rachel Tilly for president!" Sidney Wainwright called out. She was standing next to Rachel. She held up a glittery T-shirt.

Michelle's heart sank as the group let out a big cheer. "Ra-chel, Ra-chel, Ra-chel," they all chanted.

Michelle didn't know what to do. She was out of the race before it had even started!

Chapter
4

♥   "Maybe T-shirts aren't such a bad idea, Comet," Michelle told her dog after school.

Comet wagged his tail as Michelle stretched out on the living room rug. "But my allowance would never pay for them."

Joey came into the living room. "What's this about T-shirts?" he asked.

"For the election," Michelle explained, sitting up. "I really need them, but I can't afford them."

"That's what you think," Joey said with a grin. He knelt down and petted Comet.

"What do you mean?" Michelle asked.

"I'm working at a comedy club called Big Joke," Joey explained. "If you print the name of the place on the back of your shirts, they'll pay the whole bill."

"No way!" Michelle gasped.

Joey nodded. "It's called sponsoring. The club does it all the time."

"Will they do it for me?" Michelle asked.

"If they can do it for my softball team, the Mighty Yuks," Joey replied. "They can do it for anyone."

"Yippee-skippee!" Michelle shouted, jumping up. But then she thought of something. "I'm going to need the T-shirts really soon. Rachel already handed hers out."

"No problemo," Joey said. "Tony's T-Shirts can have them ready overnight."

"Great!" Michelle cried. "I want them to say MICHELLE IS A WINNER—in big letters!"

"Anything else?" Joey asked.

Michelle tapped her chin. "I'll need fifty shirts."

Joey nodded. "Anything else?"

"Silver and gold glitter?" Michelle asked hopefully.

Joey shook his head. "No can do."

"That's okay," Michelle said. "It'll be great just to have T-shirts."

"I'll take care of everything at the club," Joey said. He walked to the front door and opened it. "You can pick up your shirts on your way to school tomorrow."

"Yay!" Michelle cried. "You're the greatest, Uncle Joey."

She knelt down and hugged Comet around his furry neck. "Rachel Tilly doesn't know who she's up against!"

The next morning Danny drove Michelle to Tony's T-shirts. Danny waited in the car. And Michelle ran inside the shop.

Dozens of brightly colored T-shirts hung from the ceiling and lined the walls. A man with dark hair stood behind a counter.

"Hello," Michelle said. "Are you Tony?"

"That's me," Tony replied.

Michelle put her hands on the glass counter. "I'm here to pick up fifty T-shirts. Joey Gladstone put in my order."

"Joey's a great guy," Tony said. "The other day he told me a joke. What do pickles say when they get married?"

"I don't know." Michelle shrugged. "What?"

"Dilly beloved!" Tony laughed. "Get it? Get it?"

Michelle giggled. That definitely sounds like one of Joey's jokes, she thought. Then she glanced at the clock. Uh-oh. She was going to be late for school!

"Are my T-shirts ready?" she asked Tony.

Tony reached under the counter and pulled

out two shopping bags. "Ready or not—here they come."

"Cool," Michelle said. She picked up the two shopping bags filled with white shirts. They weren't very heavy.

"Hey," Tony said. "Don't you want to check them out first?"

"There's no time," Michelle said, running toward the door. "Thanks, Tony!"

Michelle climbed back into Danny's car. He drove her to school.

"Have a great day," Danny called as Michelle stepped out of the car.

"Oh, I will, Dad," Michelle said. She lifted both bags. "Especially with these."

Michelle ran into the school yard. She placed the shopping bags on the ground. Then she pulled out some T-shirts and handed them out. "Vote for me in the fourth-grade election," Michelle called as she tossed the shirts left and right.

Rose Wilcox and Vicky Soto walked over. They were in Mr. Dixon's fourth-grade class.

"Hi, Rose," Michelle said. "Hi, Vicky. What's up?"

Rose's eyes were shining. "José told us that you were going to ask your uncle about tickets to the Ginger Girls concert."

"Did you ask him yet?" Vicky said excitedly.

Michelle bit her lip. She had forgotten *again!* "Oops. I was too busy thinking about these." She pointed to the bags.

"Well, when you ask him," Rose said, "can you find out if he can get us tickets, too? Please?"

Vicky put her hands together. "Pretty please?"

Michelle nodded. "Sure."

"Thanks, Michelle," Rose said.

"You're the best," Vicky added.

The two girls skipped away.

Back to the T-shirts, Michelle thought. She reached into her shopping bag and pulled one out. "Michelle Tanner for fourth-grade class president!" she shouted. "Get your T-shirts here!"

Michelle felt someone tug at her jacket. She glanced over her shoulder. Victor Velez was standing behind her. He had a worried look on his face.

"Um, Michelle?" Victor said. "I wouldn't hand out those T-shirts if I were you."

"What do you mean?" Michelle asked. She rolled a T-shirt in a ball and tossed it over to Jeff Farrington. "Why not?"

Victor cleared his throat. He picked up a shirt and shook it out. "Read it," he said.

Michelle read the words on the front of the shirt. MICHELLE IS A . . . She looked at Victor. "They forgot the word *winner!*" she cried.

Then Victor flipped over the T-shirt.

Michelle read the words on the back. BIG JOKE
. . . She gasped.

"Michelle is a big joke!" Jeff cried.

"She sure is." Rachel picked up a shirt and
laughed.

Michelle wanted to disappear. She wanted
to take back all the T-shirts, but she couldn't
even move.

"This is awful!" Cassie said, running over to
Michelle. Mandy followed close behind.
"How did it happen?"

"They forgot to print the word *winner*."
Michelle said. "And the name of Joey's comedy club is *Big Joke*."

Michelle watched in horror as the kids on
the playground laughed and laughed. The joke
was definitely on her!

♥ "It was so awful," Michelle said at dinner. She told her family what happened at school. Then she turned to Joey. "It didn't happen to the Mighty Yuks—why did it have to happen to me?"

Joey shook his head. "I don't know, Michelle. Tony never messed up before."

"This will make you feel better, Michelle," Danny said. He placed a casserole on the table. "I baked a lasagna to celebrate your campaign. See? It's red, white, and blue."

Michelle stared at the lasagna. She knew

stuff was tomato sauce. And that stuff was cheese. But she was afraid sk what the *blue* stuff was. "Thanks, Dad. It looks, um, yummy."

"Great," Danny dropped a chunk of lasagna on Michelle's plate. "Now, dig in, Michelle. I know you fourth-graders have humongous appetites."

Michelle picked at her lasagna. Her appetite wasn't very big today.

"I think you need a joke, Michelle," Joey said. "What do pickles say when they get married?"

Michelle sighed. "Dilly beloved."

"How'd you know?" Joey asked, surprised.

"Aw, cheer up, Michelle," Uncle Jesse said. "Embarrassing things happen to everybody. One time I had a piece of spinach stuck on my tooth. I walked around with a green tooth all day before someone finally told me."

"Everything will be fine, Michelle," Aunt

Becky said. "And you don't need a T-shirt to let everyone know you're a winner."

"Thanks, Aunt Becky," Michelle said. "But if I'm supposed to be a winner—why do I feel like such a *loser?*"

"You are *not* a loser, Michelle," Danny insisted.

D.J. scooped out a heap of lasagna. She dropped it on her own plate. "You're not thinking of dropping out of the race, are you?" she asked.

Michelle wasn't sure. She was really embarrassed. But if she quit the election, then Rachel might win. And all Rachel cared about was putting on a show.

Victor might make a good president, she thought. But he was so quiet. Michelle wasn't even sure what Victor's plans for the fourth grade were.

Michelle shook her head. "I don't want to drop out," she told D.J. "I just don't know what to do next."

"Hey, I have an idea," Stephanie told Michelle. "Why don't you bake cookies for the kids in your school. I can give you my recipe for killer chunky pecan-banana crunch."

Nicky and Alex jumped up in their chairs.

"Cookies!" Nicky squealed.

"Yay!" Alex cheered.

"See?" Stephanie said. She pointed to the twins. "It's working already."

Michelle gave it a thought. Everybody loved cookies. Especially Stephanie's chunky pecan-banana crunch.

My ideas are the most important part of my campaign, she reminded herself. The cookies will just be a little treat. Like a goody bag at a birthday party!

"Thanks, Steph," Michelle said. "I'll get cooking right after dinner."

"And we'll all help you," Danny added. "Remember, you're not allowed to use the oven by yourself. How many cookies do you need?" he asked.

"Not many," Michelle said. "Just one hundred and fifty."

Stephanie sputtered out her milk.

"One hundred and fifty?" Danny cried.

"Hey," Michelle said. She gave a little shrug. "Fourth-graders have humongous appetites!"

Michelle trudged onto the bus the next morning. She carried a long, flat cardboard box in her arms.

"Hi, Michelle," Mandy said from her seat on the bus.

"What's that?" Cassie asked. She was sitting next to Mandy.

Michelle sat behind her friends. "I made cookies," she explained. "Chunky pecan-banana crunch. To make up for yesterday's T-shirt trouble." She carefully placed the box next to her on the seat.

"Speaking of trouble," Mandy whispered, "here comes Jeff Farrington."

Michelle saw Jeff walking toward them. "What's in the box?" he asked. "Ginger Girls tickets?"

"Jeff," Al called out. "There's no standing on the bus. Sit down, please."

"Okay," Jeff called back. He moved to sit in the seat across from Michelle.

The bus gave a little lurch.

Jeff stumbled forward. "W-w-whoa!"

Michelle gasped. "Noooo!" she cried. "Don't fall on my chunky pecan-banana—"

CRUNCH!

Chapter 6

♥ "You crushed them!" Michelle cried. "You crushed my chunky pecan-banana crunch cookies!"

Jeff wiggled off the box. "Sorry, Michelle. I didn't mean it." Then he cracked a little grin. "I guess that's the way the cookie crumbles, right?"

"Right," Michelle said with a sigh.

When they reached the school, Michelle carried her crushed cookies off the bus.

"I'm sure they're not totally ruined," Cassie said.

"Yeah," Mandy said. "Crushed cookie crumbs are great on ice cream sundaes. Maybe tomorrow you can bring in ice cream."

Michelle was so upset, she couldn't speak. She had worked so hard baking the cookies. And now they were ruined.

The girls kept walking until they were on the playground. Then Michelle stopped. She couldn't believe her eyes.

"What is it, Michelle?" Cassie asked.

"L-l-look!" Michelle stammered.

A long table stood in the middle of the school yard. It was covered with a white tablecloth and the yummiest-looking French pastries Michelle had ever seen. A sign in front of the table read VOTE FOR RACHEL.

"Eclairs!" Cassie gasped. "Cream puffs!"

"Chocolate tarts!" Mandy crooned.

Rachel was standing behind the table. She wore a black beret and a small scarf around her neck.

"Bonjour!" she called as she handed out the pastries. "That means 'hello' in French. Don't forget to vote for me!"

Now I've seen everything, Michelle thought.

"Since when is she French?" Cassie demanded.

"Who cares?" Mandy muttered. "Her dad makes the best pastries in San Francisco."

Michelle sighed. Now her cookies *really* seemed useless. She carried the box toward the trash can.

"Michelle!" a girl called.

Michelle glanced up. A group of fourth-grade girls were coming her way. They all wore Ginger Girls pins on their jackets.

"Rose called me last night," Karlee Johnson said. Karlee was in Michelle's class. "When she told me the news, I did cartwheels all over my house!"

"Is it true, Michelle?" Heather Tate asked.

41

She was in Mr. Dixon's class. "Can your uncle really get tickets for the Ginger Girls concert?"

Michelle's shoulders dropped. She was so busy baking cookies that she forgot to ask Uncle Jesse *again!*

"I didn't ask him yet," Michelle said. "But I will ask him first thing tonight."

The girls jumped up and down in a circle. When they finished shrieking, they all turned to Michelle.

"Can you get us tickets, Michelle?" Anna Abdul asked. She shook Michelle's arm. "Pleeeeeeze?"

Michelle stared at the four girls. "All of you?"

The girls nodded and smiled.

"That would be *so* cool, Michelle!" Dee Wolsky said. She was in Mr. Dixon's class, too.

"And we're starting up a Ginger Girls fan club," Heather declared. She pointed to her button. It had a picture of Gigi on it. "Do you guys want to be in it?" she asked Michelle, Cassie, and Mandy.

"That's a great idea," Michelle said.

Cassie and Mandy nodded. "An *awesome* idea," they added.

"I'll make sure to ask my uncle about the tickets." Michelle held out the box. "Want some pecan-banana cookie crumbs?"

The girls looked at the box. Then they shook their heads.

"No, thanks," Heather said. "From now on, we can eat only *ginger* cookies."

"Club rule." Dee smiled.

The girls giggled excitedly as they walked away.

Michelle shifted her box of cookie crumbs in her arms. "I hope I don't forget to ask Uncle Jesse again tonight."

"Why don't you tie a string around your finger so you won't forget?" Cassie suggested.

"Good idea," Michelle said. She tossed the box of cookie crumbs into the trash can. Then she looked through her backpack for a string.

"Michelle?" Mandy asked.

"Yes?" Michelle replied. She was still searching for a string.

Mandy smiled. "I'm kind of hungry. Would it be tacky if I got one of Rachel's cream puffs?"

"Mandy!" Michelle looked up. "Whose side are you on?" Then she spotted Victor running toward them.

"I heard that Rachel has a campaign song," Victor said, out of breath. He was holding some colorful flyers. They said VOTE FOR VICTOR on them. "She's singing it in the school yard tomorrow morning."

"A song?" Michelle groaned. "Weren't the T-shirts and French pastries enough?"

"Nothing is enough for Rachel," Victor sighed. Then he pointed to his flyers. "I've got to hand these out," he said, and ran toward the school.

"Too bad we don't have a campaign song, too," Cassie said.

"Yeah," Michelle agreed. But then she smiled slowly. "Who says I *don't* have a campaign song? My uncle Jesse started singing one at the dinner table just the other day. It's called 'Michelle Is Swell.'"

"'Michelle Is Swell,'" Mandy repeated. She nodded and smiled. "I like it. I like it!"

"Would your uncle sing it in the school yard?" Cassie asked.

"My uncle Jesse will sing *anywhere*," Michelle replied.

The school bell rang, and the girls headed for the door. Michelle glanced at Rachel, who was packing up her pastries.

Rachel may have great cream puffs, Michelle thought. But I've got a rock and rollin' uncle. Let's see her top that!

Chapter

7

♥ "Are you ready?" Uncle Jesse called from the hallway that evening.

"Ready when you are, Uncle Jesse!" Michelle was sitting on a chair in the living room. She couldn't wait for Uncle Jesse to sing her entire campaign song.

Michelle heard a loud twang from a guitar. Then Uncle Jesse jumped into the room.

Michelle giggled. Uncle Jesse was dressed in a black leather jacket and pants. His hair was slicked back, and he was wearing dark sunglasses. He looked just like his favorite singer, Elvis Presley!

"I'm not here to jive. I'm not here to sell," Uncle Jesse sang. "I'm just here to tell you that Michelle is swell." He wiggled his hips. "Michelle is swell—oh, yeah. Michelle is swell—oh, yeah . . ."

When the song was over, Michelle jumped up and down. "It's perfect, Uncle Jesse!" she cried. "Will you sing it in the school yard tomorrow morning?"

"Sure," Uncle Jesse said. "Right after I sing it in the shower."

"Oh, Uncle Jesse." Michelle threw her arms around his waist. "You're the coolest uncle in the whole world!"

Uncle Jesse curled his lip Elvis-style. "Thank you," he said. "Thank you very much."

"Is the song really that good?" Cassie asked Michelle in the school yard the next morning.

"It's excellent," Michelle declared. She

glanced at her watch. "And Uncle Jesse will be here any minute."

"I wonder what Rachel's song sounds like," Mandy said.

"I know." Cassie giggled. "Rachel Tilly is really silly!"

The three girls laughed. But then they heard the loud blast of a boom box. "What's that?" Mandy asked.

Michelle had no idea. She turned and saw four boys strutting through the school yard. They were wearing baggy pants and baseball caps. The boys pranced over to Rachel. One of them held a big radio on his shoulder. He placed the boom box on the ground. Then the boys began to rap:

"'Yo! Those of you who haven't heard—Rachel Tilly is the word!'"

"Check it out," Rachel said. She folded her arms across her chest and nodded.

"Oh, brother," Michelle said.

"Brother is right," Cassie replied. "That boy in the striped shirt is Rachel's brother, Michael."

Mandy smiled. "Really? He rocks!"

Cassie gave Mandy a shove.

"I mean—he's okay," Mandy said quickly.

A crowd of kids gathered around Rachel and her brother's group. They pumped their fists and bounced to the beat.

I'm not worried, Michelle thought. When Uncle Jesse shows up, he'll steal the show!

Cassie tugged at Michelle's jacket and pointed. "Isn't that your dad coming into the school yard?"

"My *dad?*" Michelle asked. She looked to see where Cassie was pointing.

Danny Tanner strolled into the school yard. He was wearing plaid pants, a dark green V-neck sweater, and a bow tie. A bright red kazoo was in his hand.

"Hi, Michelle!" Danny waved his kazoo.

"Dad!" Michelle said. "What are you doing here? Where's Uncle Jesse?"

"I have bad news, Michelle," Danny said. "Uncle Jesse lost his voice this morning."

"Lost his voice?" Michelle exclaimed. "Well, tell him to find it!"

"Don't worry, honey," Danny said. He twirled his kazoo. "I took some time off from work. Just so I can sing a little campaign song for the kids."

"You?" Michelle gasped.

Danny smiled as he walked toward the playground.

"No! No!" Michelle cried. She ran after her father. "Dad—please, don't!"

But it was too late. Danny sat down on a seesaw and blew a note into his kazoo. "Gather around me boys and girls," he called out. "I'd like to sing a ditty about a very special little girl. And I think you know who she is."

Danny tweaked another note on the kazoo.

Then he began to sing: " 'Oh, the kids on the bus say, Michelle is swell . . . Michelle is swell . . . Michelle is swell!' "

Michelle heard some kids in the school yard snicker. She squeezed her eyes shut. This was *not* the campaign song she had in mind.

"Um, it's not so bad, Michelle," Cassie said. She touched Michelle's shoulder.

"Yeah," Mandy added. "The kindergarten kids really like it."

Then Michelle heard Rachel and her brother laughing loudly behind her.

"Who's the dude with the kazoo?" Michael asked.

"That's Michelle Tanner's dad," Rachel replied, giggling. "Is he corny or what?"

Michelle felt her cheeks burn. How dare Rachel insult her dad! She whirled around. "At least my dad is on TV every morning," Michelle told Rachel. "He's the host of *Wake Up, San Francisco.*"

"Big deal." Rachel sneered. "At least my dad's not a nerd! Only *nerds* play the kazoo!"

Cassie pulled Michelle away. "Come on, Michelle. Forget about her."

But Michelle couldn't forget. Rachel had gone too far. That does it, she thought. From now on, no more Miss Nice Girl!

Chapter
8

♥ Michelle sat on her favorite swing during recess. But she wasn't swinging. She was watching Mandy and Cassie ask the fourth-graders who they would vote for.

"Well?" Michelle asked when her friends had finished. She jumped off the swing. "What did you find out?"

Cassie and Mandy glanced at each other.

"Um," Cassie said. "No big deal."

"Yeah," Mandy said. "Some kids are voting for Rachel. And some kids are voting for you."

Michelle gave a little hop. "Really?" she

asked excitedly. "How many kids are voting for me?"

Mandy stared at her sneakers. "Seven," she said softly.

Michelle's shoulders slumped. There were fifty kids in the whole fourth grade!

"You mean everyone else is voting for Rachel?" Michelle demanded.

"No," Mandy said. "Not everyone."

"About twelve are voting for Victor," Cassie said.

Michelle's eyes widened. "I can't believe it." She leaned against the monkey bars. "Even Victor is ahead of me. Shy, quiet Victor!"

"Don't worry, Michelle," Mandy said. She waved her hand. "This was a totally dumb idea. Whose idea was it anyway?"

"Yours," Cassie replied.

Mandy blushed. "Oh, yeah."

Michelle felt awful. Rachel and Sidney were headed her way. That made it even worse.

"Hi, Michelle," Rachel said. She ran her fingers through her super-long hair. "I heard nobody is going to vote for you."

"That's not true," Michelle said. Seven people were voting for me, she thought.

"Now is a good time to quit," Sidney said. "Don't you think?"

Michelle clenched her fists. "The race for class president isn't over—until the last vote is counted."

Rachel and Sidney shrugged their shoulders. Then they strolled away.

"What are you going to do now, Michelle?" Cassie asked.

"You'll see," Michelle said. She marched to the monkey bars and climbed halfway to the top. "If you vote for me, you won't be sorry!" she shouted.

A few kids looked up.

"What will you do?" Lee Wagner asked.

Michelle thought of her usual promises. The

videos in the library and the class picnic didn't seem to work. She had to think of something else. "I'll . . . I'll . . . make sure there's colored chalk in all the classrooms!"

The kids looked at each other. "We already have colored chalk," a girl said.

"Wait!" Michelle said as the kids began to leave. "I'll make sure there's root beer in all the water fountains!"

The kids turned around.

"Oh, yeah?" Lucas Hamilton said.

"Not only that," Michelle went on. "There'll be movies in the lunchroom. And birthday cake for lunch every week. It's got to be *some-one's* birthday every week."

More kids came over to listen.

"And," Michelle continued, "I'll make sure there is no homework again. Ever!"

"No homework?" Evan Burger cheered. "Way to go!"

"I'm voting for Michelle," Denise Chow said.

"Me, too!"

"So am I!"

The school bell rang. The kids buzzed with excitement as they headed to their class-rooms.

Later, Michelle's class took a spelling test. Then Mrs. Yoshida passed out some papers. "Here is your new vocabulary list," she said. "For homework I want you to look up each word in the dictionary."

The class groaned as Mrs. Yoshida wrote the homework assignment on the board.

"But it's Friday," Lee Wagner complained.

"And there are twelve words on this list," Erin whispered.

"I can't wait until Michelle is class president," Jeff said in a loud voice. "Then we won't have any more homework."

Mrs. Yoshida stopped writing on the board. She turned around. "What's this about no homework, Michelle?"

Michelle stared at Mrs. Yoshida. She didn't know what to say. "Um . . . I . . . er . . . um."

Then the door swung open. A fifth-grade monitor stepped in. "Will Michelle Tanner please come to the principal's office?" he announced.

Michelle froze. Uh-oh. What did I do?

Chapter 9

 "I heard you made some promises on the playground today," Mr. Posey said. He folded his hands on his desk and looked at Michelle.

Michelle sat on a chair facing the principal's desk. "Yes, Mr. Posey."

Mr. Posey sighed as he studied a sheet of paper. "The root beer in the water fountain is bad enough," he said. "But can you imagine a school day without homework?"

Michelle gave it a thought. She could imagine a day without homework. It would be pretty cool.

Mr. Posey leaned back in his chair. "A day without homework would be like—a cake without the frosting," he said. "Like a hot dog without the bun. Like a parade without the floats. Can you imagine a parade without the floats, Michelle?"

"But I promised those things only so I could win the election, Mr. Posey," Michelle said. "Besides, I had to do it. Rachel was handing out T-shirts, pastries—she even had a campaign song!"

Mr. Posey tilted his head and smiled. "Just like *you* did, Michelle?"

Mr. Posey is right, she thought. I *was* doing everything Rachel was doing—just to win votes. I even forgot about my great ideas. What was I *thinking?*

"Sorry, Mr. Posey." Michelle sighed. "I'll never make another bad promise again."

And I won't be like Rachel ever again, she thought.

Michelle spent the weekend working on her speech for the special assembly on Monday. She wrote it over and over again. She even practiced saying it to Comet and her guinea pig, Sunny.

When Monday came, Michelle was ready!

Mrs. Yoshida's class filed into the auditorium. Michelle took a seat on the stage. Sitting to her left was Rachel. On her right was Victor.

"Good luck, Victor," Michelle said. She glanced to Rachel. I'm going to be a good sport, she decided. "Good luck," she told Rachel.

"Good morning, boys and girls," Mr. Posey said to the fourth-grade classes. "As you can see, our three candidates are ready to share their speeches with us."

Michelle's knees were shaking. She clutched her speech so tightly that the paper almost ripped.

"We'll go in birthday order," Mr. Posey

said. "And since Victor's birthday is in January, he'll go first."

Victor stood up and walked to the microphone. A teacher lowered it to his size.

Victor cleared his throat. "Hi," he said. He held his speech in front of him. "My name is Victor. But you probably know me as the kid no one wants on their kick-ball team."

The auditorium laughed. Michelle smiled, too.

"Okay, okay." Victor held up his hands. "I may not be great at kick-ball, but I do know what fourth-graders want and need. We need new art supplies. Our jars of paints are dried up, and our paintbrushes are crusty."

Hmm, Michelle thought. Victor's right.

"We also need more bulletin board space in the hall," Victor said. "And a fourth-grade glee club. Why should we have to wait until fifth grade to sing? We've got plenty to sing about right now!"

"Yeah!" a girl shouted.

"Right on!" a boy called out.

"Anyway," Victor said. "Vote for me, for a new and better fourth grade. And while you're at it, pick me for kick ball, too. I'm not *that* bad!"

The kids clapped and laughed at Victor's joke.

Wow, Michelle thought. I didn't know Victor would make such a good president. If I weren't running, I'd vote for him.

"Thank you, Victor," Mr. Posey said. "Rachel's birthday comes next, and so does her speech. Rachel?"

Rachel stood up and walked to the microphone. She was wearing black pants and a red beaded sweater. Her hair was pulled back into a sleek ponytail.

"Good morning, fellow fourth-graders," Rachel said. "As you probably all know, I'm Rachel Tilly."

Michelle could see Mandy rolling her eyes.

"I thought this election was going to be a challenge," Rachel continued. "Until I found out Michelle Tanner was running, too."

Michelle's mouth dropped open. Huh?

"Michelle acts like she's everybody's friend," Rachel said. "But there's a lot more to Michelle Tanner than meets the eye."

Michelle couldn't believe it. Rachel was about to trash her—in front of the whole fourth grade!

"Just last month Michelle was stopped for running in the hall," Rachel told the auditorium. "On the same day she turned in a library book a day late. I know—I was standing right behind her."

It's not true, it's not true, Michelle thought. I was absent the day the book was due. And I was running in the hall the next day to return it!

"Running in the hall, late library books,"

Rachel repeated. She pointed her finger at Michelle. "Is *that* the person you want as your class president?"

The auditorium was silent as Rachel took her seat.

"Your turn, Michelle," Rachel said sweetly.

"Michelle?" Mr. Posey said. "Would you like to read your speech?"

Michelle stood up and walked to the microphone. She wanted to say mean things about Rachel—just as Rachel had done to her. But Michelle knew that would be wrong. And she didn't want to be like Rachel anymore.

Michelle also knew that she had to do something that was going to be very hard. She had to take back all of her bad promises.

"Good morning," Michelle said. She forced herself to smile. "The promises I made about the root beer in the water fountains and no homework were promises I cannot keep."

Groans filled the auditorium.

"Instead," Michelle went on, "I promise to be the best fourth-grade class president I can. You all know what a hard worker I am. And I know I can make a difference in this school. I mean it when I say that I will try to get us more school trips. Getting more books and videos in the library is important. And I think it's time fourth-graders got to use the cool playground!"

Applause filled the auditorium.

Michelle took a deep breath. "But most of all, I will never make a promise that I can't keep. Thank you."

Michelle felt proud of her speech. But she was glad it was over. She turned to take her seat on the stage.

Then a boy jumped out of his seat. "Liar!" he cried out. "You're a big liar!"

Chapter

10

♥ Michelle froze. She couldn't believe her ears. I am *not* a liar! she thought. I meant everything I said!

Then Robert Lopez from Mrs. Barnett's class pointed to Cindy Sherman in the next seat. "Liar!" Robert shouted. "You're not getting tickets to the Ginger Girls concert. There are no tickets left anywhere!"

Cindy jumped up. "I am so," she insisted. "My dad works for a record company and he already has them."

"Nuh-uh!" Robert said.

"Uh-huh!" Cindy said.

"Nuh-uh!"

"Uh-huh!"

"Kids, kids!" Mr. Posey said into the mike. "Settle down."

Whew, Michelle thought. This isn't about me. It's about the Ginger Girls! She took her seat.

"Great speech, Michelle," Victor whispered. "I liked your idea about more books in the library."

Rachel pushed her chair closer to Michelle and Victor. "Why? So she can hand them in *late?*"

Michelle ignored Rachel. She leaned back in her seat and sighed. Her speech was over. Now it was up to the fourth-grade class to pick a president.

"Just think," Mandy told Cassie. "At this time tomorrow we might be eating lunch with the president of the fourth grade!"

The only thing that would be better is if the Ginger Girls had a concert right here at our school," Cassie said.

"What do you think, Michelle?" Mandy asked with a little giggle. "Can your uncle set it up?"

Michelle was so nervous. She couldn't even think about the Ginger Girls. "I still have an awful feeling that Rachel might win," she said.

"Why?" Cassie cried. "You're the one with the awesome ideas. And you gave a great speech today."

"Thanks," Michelle said. "But Rachel gave out cool T-shirts, yummy pastries, and her campaign song rocked. What if the kids vote for her just for that?"

"Michelle Tanner," Mandy shook her finger. "That is stinkin' thinkin'!"

"Stinkin' thinkin'?" Michelle repeated.

Mandy nodded. "You have to think positive all the time."

"You're right, Mandy." Michelle nodded. "Besides, what does Rachel Tilly have that I don't have?"

"Yo-yos," Cassie said flatly.

Michelle turned to Cassie. "Huh?"

"Rachel is handing out light-up yo-yos," Cassie explained. She used her tuna sandwich to point across the lunchroom.

Michelle saw Rachel standing on a table. She was tossing yo-yos to a crowd of kids.

"The yo-yos have my name on them," Rachel said. "So you'll all remember who to vote for tomorrow."

"Oh, great." Michelle flopped her head on the table.

"Come on," Cassie said. She waved her hand at her friends. "This I've got to see."

Michelle, Cassie, and Mandy joined the crowd in front of Rachel.

"If I'm elected class president, I'll make sure the fourth grade has their own school bus!" Rachel shouted as she tossed out yo-yos. "And every seat will be a window seat!"

Michelle shook her head. Rachel wasn't just handing out yo-yos. She was making big promises.

"If I'm elected class president," Rachel went on, "the fourth grade will go to the beach at least once a month. I'll even have my dad bake us bear claws every Friday!"

Mandy stood on her toes. She cupped her hands around her mouth. "Who cares?" she yelled. "If Michelle is elected, she'll have the Ginger Girls sing at our assembly!"

Michelle's eyes popped open. She stared at Mandy. *"What* did you just say?"

"Whoops!" Mandy said. She clapped her hand over her mouth.

The crowd turned and stared at Michelle.

"Is it true, Michelle?" Lucas asked. "Will you really have the Ginger Girls sing at our assembly?"

"I . . . uh," Michelle stammered. She glanced around the lunchroom. All the kids were staring at her. Michelle didn't know what to say. But she knew that she had to say something— fast.

Chapter

11

♥ Are the Ginger Girls really singing at our assembly?" Jamar patted Michelle on the back. "That would be so cool."

Michelle's face grew hot. All the kids in the lunchroom stared at her. She wanted to tell them the Ginger Girls were coming to their school. But then she remembered what she had said in her speech. About not making any more bad promises.

And I meant it, Michelle thought. She knew what she had to say. "I'm sorry. I can't promise the Ginger Girls," Michelle told the boys and girls.

The kids groaned.

"I knew it!" Rachel chirped. She tossed a yo-yo to another boy. "Michelle could never keep a big promise like that."

"At least I told the truth," Michelle replied. She folded her arms across her chest.

"Give me a break." Sidney hung her arm around Rachel's shoulders. "You can't get the fourth grade any good stuff. More books and videos in the library? Who cares about that?"

"I do!" Mandy cried out.

"Me, too," Cassie said.

"So do I," Lee Wagner said. He tossed his yo-yo back to Rachel. A few other kids did the same.

"Come on," Michelle told Cassie and Mandy. "Let's go."

The three friends walked back to their lunch table by the window. They sat quietly for a while.

Then Michelle turned to Mandy. "Why did

you say I could get the Ginger Girls to come to our school? I could never keep a promise like that. Not in a million years."

"Michelle's right," Cassie agreed. "The Ginger Girls would never come to our school."

"I'm sorry," Mandy said. "Rachel was making me so mad. It just slipped out. I didn't mean to say it."

Michelle nodded. "I know. It's okay," she replied. "Besides, Rachel is probably going to win the election anyway. You saw how those kids went for her yo-yos."

"I have an idea," Mandy said. "Why don't you talk to your uncle Jesse about the Ginger Girls. You never *did* ask him if he knows them. Maybe he *does*. And maybe he can get them to sing at our school."

"But that won't help us win the election," Cassie said.

"Cassie's right," Michelle agreed. "We vote tomorrow."

"But it would still be awesome if you got the Ginger Girls to sing at our school," Mandy said. "And Rachel and Sidney won't be able to say you can't keep a big promise. Not after that."

Michelle stared out the lunchroom window. She didn't really care what Rachel said about her. Still, it would be great if the Ginger Girls sang at an assembly.

"Okay, I'll talk to Uncle Jesse," Michelle said. "What do I have to lose?"

"How was the speech assembly?" Uncle Jesse asked Michelle after school. He was sorting out his CD collection in the living room. "Did you wow the kids with your promises?"

"Oh, I wowed them, all right." Michelle flopped onto the couch.

Jesse looked up from his CDs. "Is something wrong?"

Michelle slid onto the rug next to her uncle. Then she explained the whole story. "And then I said I couldn't get the Ginger Girls to come to our school. It's such a crazy promise."

Jesse scratched his chin. "It's a big promise, Michelle. But I'm not so sure it's that crazy."

"What do you mean?" Michelle asked

"I know a guy named Tom," Jesse explained. "He plays guitar for the Ginger Girls."

Michelle sat up straight. "Really?"

"Tom told me that he can get tickets to any of the Ginger Girls concerts," Jesse said.

Michelle jumped up. "Can he also get the Ginger Girls to sing at my school?"

"I'll call him and ask," Jesse said.

Michelle waited in the living room while Jesse made the call. When he came back he had a big smile on his face. "Good news," he announced. "Tom said that the Ginger Girls are great sports. And they love kids."

"Does that mean . . . ?" Michelle gasped.

Jesse shrugged. "He said it would be no problem!"

"Yippee!" Michelle yelled. "The Ginger Girls are coming to my school!"

The next day couldn't come fast enough for Michelle. It was finally Tuesday—Election Day!

"You'll need these to fill out the election ballots," Rachel announced before class. She passed out some pencils.

Michelle looked at one of Rachel's pencils and frowned. It read VOTE FOR RACHEL in gold letters.

One thing about Rachel, Michelle thought. She doesn't give up either.

After saying the Pledge of Allegiance, Mrs. Yoshida passed around paper ballots.

"I think I know who you're voting for." Erin smiled at Michelle.

Michelle smiled back. She checked her own name on the ballot sheet.

When everyone was finished, Mrs. Yoshida collected the ballots. "All the votes are in." She glanced at the clock on the wall. "We'll go to the election assembly right after lunch."

Michelle couldn't pay attention to Mrs. Yoshida's lessons that morning. She couldn't even eat her turkey sandwich during lunch. All she could think about was the election.

Soon Mrs. Yoshida's class filed into the auditorium.

"We'll be rooting for you, Michelle," Mandy whispered.

Michelle's stomach did a somersault. This was it. The moment she had worked so hard for all week.

Michelle, Rachel, and Victor took their seats on the stage.

"I wonder if I'll have my own page in the fourth-grade yearbook," Rachel said. "Or if I'll get a pin that says PRESIDENT."

"Good luck, Michelle," Victor whispered.

Michelle turned him. "You, too, Victor," she said.

Mr. Posey stepped up to the mike. "Before I announce the winner," he said. "I would like to say that all of your votes have been counted and tabulated by Lionel, our fifth-grade math whiz."

A few kids clapped as a boy with glasses bowed. Then he handed Mr. Posey a piece of paper. It was folded in half.

"All right," Mr. Posey said. "Who wants to know who the next fourth-grade class president will be?"

All hands in the auditorium shot up.

"Then, here goes," Mr. Posey said. He unfolded the paper and smiled. "And the fourth-grade class president is . . ."

Chapter

12

♥ Mr. Posey stared out at the audience. "This is exciting, isn't it? Are you sure you all want to know who's president?"

"Tell us, Mr. Posey," a boy called out. "Tell us!"

"Okay." Mr. Posey laughed. "The fourth-grade class president is . . ."

Rachel began to stand up.

"Michelle Tanner!" Mr. Posey announced.

THUD. Rachel fell back into her chair.

"Me?" Michelle gasped. She gazed around the auditorium. Mandy and Cassie were hugging each other. The other kids were clapping and cheering.

"You won, Michelle," Victor said. "Go up there!"

Michelle's knees felt like jelly as she walked over to the principal. "Congratulations, Michelle." Mr. Posey shook her hand. "Is there anything you'd like to say to the fourth grade?"

"Yes." Michelle turned to the microphone. "First I'd like to say thanks. Next I'd like to say that as your class president, I will stand by *all* my promises."

Rachel cleared her throat loudly. "Big deal," she said.

"And I have one more promise that I didn't tell you about," Michelle went on. "I wanted to make sure that I could keep it before I said anything."

The auditorium became silent.

Michelle smiled. "The Ginger Girls are

coming to Fraser Street Elementary!" she cried. "They're going to sing!"

A loud cheer filled the auditorium. "Michelle is swell!" the kids chanted. "Michelle is swell! Michelle is swell!"

When the cheering finally stopped, Mr. Posey turned to Michelle. "So, Michelle. How does it feel to be class president?" he asked.

"Great, Mr. Posey," Michelle replied. "But there's still one thing that I want to do."

"Oh?" Mr. Posey asked. "What's that?"

"All presidents have a vice president." Michelle pointed to Victor. "I choose Victor Velez to be mine."

"Yesssss!" Victor cheered. He jumped up and ran to Michelle's side.

"That's not fair!" Rachel marched to the front of the stage and pointed to the audience. "I want my T-shirts back. And my yo-yos! And you'll never eat my father's doughnuts again!"

Michelle smiled at Victor. They joined hands and raised them in the air.

I think I'm going to like being president, Michelle thought as she listened to the cheers. I'm going to like it a *lot*.